INNOCENT BLOOD

SINKHOLE

INNOCENT BLOOD

SUSAN KOEHLER

DARBY CREEK

MINNEAPOLIS

Darby Creek
An imprint of Lerner Publishing Group, Inc.
241 First Avenue North
Minneapolis, MN 55401 USA

For reading levels and more information, look up this title at www.lernerbooks.com.

Cover and interior images: Copyright ©2019 Kseniya Ivashkevich/Shutterstock (girl in forest); Copyright ©2013 Ricardo Reitmeyer/Shutterstock (moon); Monory/Shutterstock (fog); Milano M (chapter number background)

Main body text set in Janson Text LT Std.
Typeface provided by Adobe Systems.

Library of Congress Cataloging-in-Publication Data

Names: Koehler, Susan, 1963– author.
Title: Innocent blood / Susan Koehler.
Description: Minneapolis : Darby Creek, [2023] | Series: Sinkhole | Audience: Ages 11–18. | Audience: Grades 10–12. | Summary: Rosa Vieja learns that a local legend may explain the mysterious disappearances of her dad and her classmate.
Identifiers: LCCN 2022021425 (print) | LCCN 2022021426 (ebook) | ISBN 9781728475493 (lib. bdg.) | ISBN 9781728477961 (pbk.) | ISBN 9781728479491 (eb pdf)
Subjects: CYAC: Missing persons—Fiction. | Supernatural—Fiction. | LCGFT: Paranormal fiction. | High interest-low vocabulary books. | Novels.
Classification: LCC PZ7.1.K6732 In 2023 (print) | LCC PZ7.1.K6732 (ebook) | DDC [Fic]—dc23

LC record available at https://lccn.loc.gov/2022021425
LC ebook record available at https://lccn.loc.gov/2022021426

Manufactured in the United States of America
1 – TR – 12/15/22

Rosa is awake again, unable to silence the voices that echo in her mind. *Poor Rosa. Her dad left them. He said he was going to work and then never came back. He's such a loser.* Rosa fluffs the pillow beneath her head and rolls to her side, but the voices won't stop. *Her poor mom. She had to take on a second job at Foggy Creek Diner.* Did they think she couldn't hear the whispers? That she didn't recognize the pity in their awkward smiles? Their heads leaning together when they thought she wasn't watching? And still, she fights to keep herself from believing that the voices might be right. Maybe he just decided to leave.

It's been almost a month since Luca Vieja loaded equipment into his truck and headed out for a surveying job east of town. Nearly a month since he laid his hard hat on the passenger seat and then turned to say goodbye. Nearly a month since he smiled, his bright yellow vest gleaming in the morning sunlight, and said, "Tonight we feast! Pizza and ice cream." It was his favorite meal. And Rosa knew, beyond the shadow of a doubt, that he intended to return. So where is he?

Luca Vieja had worked as a surveyor for Dawson County and then for the state of Texas before deciding to go into business for himself. He saved money. He bought his own equipment. Rosa's mother, always the worrier, had wrung her hands and protested. Luca had taken her hands into his own and said, "This area is growing, Marisol. Soon the jobs will be like stars in the sky. More than you can imagine." He was a dreamer. He was not a deserter.

Rosa tosses and turns, her mind alive with recent history. Still so clearly, she can see the sheriff's deputies sitting on the living room sofa. She can hear her mother begging them to search. Begging for a formal missing person's report. Crying to the officers as they nod. They give her tissues. They take notes.

"If anything turns up, we'll call you." Those are the last words they say. So far, there has been only one phone call. To report they've found nothing. To ask again if there had been a fight. To ask again if perhaps there is another woman.

Rosa sits up and pushes her long brown hair away from her face. She pulls back the covers and lifts the shade. She opens the window, longing for fresh air. For movement. For relief. The night sky is lit by a waxing moon. Almost full, like it was that night. That last night she shared with her father. When they sat on the porch and wished upon stars.

Rosa shakes her head, trying to release the memories. To find peace. *So much for wishes,* she thinks. *Nothing comes of dreams and wishes.*

She turns to see Luca's photo on her bedside table. Moonlight shimmers on the glass. She lifts the frame in her hands. "Papa, where are you?" she asks. Suddenly, a tear falls from her eye, and she watches as it travels along the glass, as if rolling down her father's face. As if he cries with her.

Cradling the frame in her arms, Rosa moves to the window. The night is warm, and a gentle breeze passes lightly across her face, offering a little relief. She faces east, the direction Luca had gone. Her heart longs to see him, but her eyes find only emptiness. Beneath the nearly full moon, lifeless terrain stretches until it finally dissolves into the mist that hangs at the edge of her world.

And then it happens. At first, she thinks she imagines it. She lays the picture aside and kneels by the window, staring into the moonlight glow and listening so carefully. And then she hears it again. From somewhere beyond the barren field, somewhere within the mist. Clearly, without a doubt, she hears the words: *Innocent blood.*

Rosa stands at her locker, eyes aching and mind clouded.

"Ready for Mr. White's history test?" Manny Garcia, Rosa's best friend, has the locker next to hers. His eyes gleam with their usual excitement. Whether he's talking about a great hamburger or an upcoming test, Manny always speaks with the same bright-eyed enthusiasm.

"I'm sorry," Rosa responds. Apologies are becoming so familiar. "I was up late studying for the test. History isn't my best subject."

"You'll do great," Manny assures her. "And it's Friday! Always the best day!" Manny closes his locker and spins the combination lock three times after securing it. Just like he always does.

"It's Friday," Rosa repeats. "At least I can sleep in tomorrow."

Manny nods, encouraging her slight tilt toward the bright side. "And," he adds, "there's a football game tonight—"

"Rosa!" Manny's obvious invitation is cut off by Kyle Baron. Tall, sandy hair, green eyes, the perfect smile. Even in her sleep-deprived state, Rosa's knees go a little weak at the sound of his voice. "Are you coming to see me play tonight?"

Manny stands behind Kyle, grinning and nodding. He covers his heart and then puts a hand to his forehead as if swooning. He's hard to ignore, but Rosa does her best as Kyle continues.

"After the game, a bunch of us are getting together at that old, abandoned oil field east of town." He smiles, and his green eyes sparkle.

Rosa thinks maybe she sees the hint of a blush in his cheeks. Strands of hair have fallen onto his forehead, and Kyle tosses his head to one side to sling them away from his face.

Rosa's heart rushes. "I don't know," she hears herself say. "I need to check with my mom, but maybe." She tilts her head and smiles, clutching her books to her chest. Before she can think of anything else to say, Theresa Colon interrupts the magic moment.

"Kyle," Theresa gushes, "the bell's about to ring. We need to get to English. You know how Mrs. Garber acts if you're not in your seat when the bell rings." Theresa rolls her eyes and giggles, grabbing Kyle's elbow and dragging him away.

Kyle looks back at Rosa and winks. And over his shoulder, he yells, "See you tonight!"

"Earth to Rosa," Manny says, snapping his fingers a few times. "You need to come down out of the clouds so we can get to that history test."

"He's so nice," Rosa says, her gaze locked

until Kyle completely disappears. Then she smiles at Manny and whispers, "Don't tell anybody, but I like him."

"Oh, you think that's a secret?" Manny laughs. "So, I'll pick you up around six. If you want, we can just plan to get burgers at the game."

"Burgers," Rosa repeats. "*Your* not-so-secret crush."

The friends laugh as they walk to class, and for Rosa, a spark of life feels renewed. Just before entering Mr. White's room, Manny says, "And check with your mom about after the game. Sounds fun."

"Mama, *please*," Rosa begs. She knows she has only a few moments to talk. Her mother rushes to eat leftover lasagna after arriving home late from her day shift at Rose Grocery. "You'll be at the diner, and I'll be here all alone. Why can't I go hang out after the game?"

Marisol Vieja stops moving momentarily. She sighs. Her shoulders slouch and Rosa thinks she is about to give in. But she thinks wrong. "Rosa, do you know that tonight is the full moon?" She doesn't need to say more. Her worried expression says it all.

"Can I at least go to the game?" Rosa asks, trying her best to look pitiful and evoke sympathy.

"Manny is driving, correct?" her mother asks.

"Yes, Manny is driving," Rosa answers, still frowning, still trying to force tears into her eyes.

Marisol Vieja sighs again. "You can go to the game," she says. "And come straight home when it ends." Then she looks at her watch and adds, "My shift at the diner begins at 5:30. Do you need money to eat at the game?"

After quickly pressing a ten-dollar bill into Rosa's palm, her mother rushes out the door. Her short break has ended, and she'll be at the diner until it closes at midnight.

Rosa looks at the money in her hand and feels the familiar twinge of guilt. She had offered to get a job, but her mother had refused. She wants Rosa to focus on school, to get good grades, to make something of herself. She doesn't need the distraction of a job.

Rosa stuffs the ten dollars into the pocket of her jeans. She knows that Manny will arrive soon. She knows they will get a burger at the game and watch Kyle play. And she also knows that after the game, she will go to the abandoned oil field. As long as she's home before midnight, her mother will never know.

"Foggy Creek! Foggy Creek! Go, Foggy Creek!" Voices roar in Rosa's ears. The bleachers vibrate beneath her feet. Bright lights flood the field and give a crispness to the grass, the white lines and numbers, the goalposts. For the first time since her father's disappearance, Rosa's senses have awakened.

"Is that a smile I see?" Rosa looks at Manny, and his grin widens.

"Okay, you win," she says. "The game was a good idea." Rosa tries to push away the looming shadow of guilt. *Can you forget your father so easily? If you leave your mourning behind, you erase him.* But Rosa is determined to push through the nagging guilt and have one night of fun. *It's just a break*, she tells herself.

"Manny, my man!" Terrance Brown rouses Rosa from her internal argument. "I can't believe we still have to play a fourth quarter. We've already dominated. This game is over."

Manny stands and stretches. "Kyle is on fire!" he says. And then he cuts his eyes to Rosa, just to see her blush at the mention of Kyle Baron's name.

"The dude is unstoppable," Terrance offers, totally unaware of Rosa's presence, let alone her rush of emotions. Then Terrance adds, "I hope you're coming to the party after the game. I'm the unofficial DJ, blasting tunes from my truck."

Manny laughs. "That's something I'd like to see!"

Terrance raises his arms as if acknowledging an appreciative crowd. "Oh, yeah. The World-Renowned Terrance Brown!" It doesn't seem to matter that no one is looking, other than Manny and Rosa. He lowers his arms and leans toward Manny. "You'll be there, right?"

"Well," Manny begins, searching for words. "I'm Rosa's ride, and—"

Rosa cuts him off and finishes his sentence for him. "—Rosa just wants to be sure she's invited too." She flashes a wry smile at Manny and looks back at Terrance.

"Rosa!" Terrance puts a hand to his heart and bows. "My apologies. I didn't see you there. Of course, you're invited, girl!"

"Then it's settled," she says. "Manny and I will see you after the game."

As Terrance moves on to continue working the crowd, Manny looks at Rosa with stunned delight. "This is awesome. I can't believe your mom said yes!"

The familiar guilt returns, and Rosa pushes it back again. "She didn't exactly say yes. As a matter of fact, it was a pretty hard no."

Manny immediately holds both hands up and shakes his head. "Whoa, I don't want to be a part of getting you in trouble with your mom. She's like president of my fan club. I don't want to ruin that."

"Relax," Rosa says. "She's working tonight, and the diner doesn't close until midnight. As long as I'm home before she is, she'll never know."

Manny rolls his eyes. "So, this is like Cinderella at the ball. Is my car gonna turn into a pumpkin if I don't get you out of there before the clock strikes midnight?"

"Yeah," Rosa answers, "and you will turn into a mouse."

"We will definitely leave before midnight. I'm small enough as it is," Manny quips.

"Lucky for you, that abandoned oil field is on my side of town," Rosa assures him. "Piece of cake."

Suddenly, the crowd roars again, and the bleachers shake. Manny and Rosa jump to their feet in time to see the digital countdown clock hit zero and watch both teams head for the sidelines. The Foggy Creek players jump up and down in victory, holding their helmets aloft. Suddenly, Kyle is lifted in the air, the classic salute to a battlefield champion. Again, Rosa blushes. And her heart glows in anticipation of the night that lay ahead.

Manny and Rosa gather their trash and inch along with the crowd. The mood is joyful and victorious, and Rosa soaks it in. There, beneath the lights, shoulder to shoulder with humanity, she feels alive again.

But as they walk to Manny's car, the stadium lights fade, the crowd breaks off in multiple directions, and Rosa's footsteps grow heavy. Once more, she fights to ignore the guilt that keeps resurfacing. Before climbing into Manny's car, she looks to the east, knowing that somewhere in the distance is her home, the museum of her memories. And beyond that, there is the abandoned oil field, which just might prove to be a place of new beginnings.

Of course, the only thing Rosa can see in the distance is a thickening blanket of fog beneath the full moon. She shudders and climbs into the car.

Manny's car bumps along the rough terrain, and Rosa prays she won't be sick when they finally reach the party. She imagines it a little too clearly. *Oh, hi Kyle . . . vomit.* She shakes her head, stiffens her resolve, and presses her body against the seat.

"Off-roading!" Manny shouts. "This is wild!" He slaps the dash and laughs, undoubtedly enjoying this experience far more than Rosa.

Soon, they are surrounded by headlights. Lots of headlights. Cars and trucks line opposite sides of an open field, each blasting light across the open space. It's almost like being in the stadium again, except for the fog. And the music. The really loud music.

Manny's car finally rolls to a stop. He turns the engine off but keeps the lights on. "Good thing I have jumper cables," he says. "I have a feeling a few batteries aren't going to make it through this party."

Rosa is suddenly anxious. She needs to count on Manny's car. She can't be late. It isn't a pumpkin or a mouse she fears; it's her mother.

Manny senses her alarm. "Don't worry," he says. "My battery will be fine. Plus, I'll turn the engine on a half hour before we need to go. Really, it'll be fine."

Manny and Rosa climb from the car and enter the grassy dance floor. A low fog gives off the appearance of dry ice. To one side of the field, more cars come, edging along the bumpy road. The other side is a mystery, shrouded by mist and darkness. Rosa shudders, suddenly remembering the voice . . . *Innocent blood.*

Standing here now, surrounded by bodies and headlights, she feels silly. Maybe she hadn't actually been awake after all. Maybe the whole thing was a dream.

Suddenly, the music changes. A new song, a new sound. Rosa shakes away the memory of the dream—*it had to have been a dream*—and returns to the present.

She watches as Terrance hops down from the bed of his truck and joins the bouncing, swaying, dancing bodies. He spots Manny and yells, "New subwoofers! Gotta love that sound!" He howls to the moonlight, and Manny laughs.

Then Manny turns to Rosa and says, "Terrance Brown, world renowned . . . wolf." Rosa laughs politely, but she's distracted, her eyes searching the crowd.

Manny sighs. "Give it a rest," he says. "The players will be the last to arrive. You know, debrief, showers . . ."

Rosa rolls her eyes, unaware that Theresa is standing beside her. "You two make the cutest couple," Theresa says, startling Rosa and throwing her off her guard. "Look," Theresa says to her small posse of friends, "don't Manny and Rosa make a cute couple?"

"We're just friends," Rosa clarifies.

Manny follows up, flashing a bright smile. "That's right, ladies. I am 100 percent available. Who wants to dance?"

The girls giggle, except for Theresa, and Manny takes one of them by the hand and begins to dance. Rosa must look away from his embarrassing dance moves. He spins, drops, poses, and looks completely ridiculous. But he doesn't seem to mind. And neither does his dance partner.

Suddenly, more lights bounce into sight, and the crowd erupts with cheers. A small caravan of vehicles lines up alongside the others, and the guests of honor step onto the field.

"Kyle!" Theresa yells, waving and jumping, and suddenly she's gone. Rosa stands alone for the moment, knowing that as much as Theresa tries to divert Kyle's attention, she won't win.

He always seems to find his way to Rosa. She smiles at the thought.

Quarterback Rick Santini jumps on the hood of a car, lifting a football above his head, and the crowd cheers with wild abandon. A senior, Santini's been weighing college offers as if he owns the future. Must be nice, Rosa thinks.

As she holds her place and watches, Kyle Baron makes his way through the crowd. High fives, chest bumps, head slaps, you name it. Everyone must touch him, as if his prowess, his greatness, will rub off on them. Kyle Baron is golden. And he's making his way toward Rosa.

Of course, Theresa hovers at his side, and then hops in front of him, walking backwards, trying to establish eye contact. Anything to get his attention. *Pathetic*, Rosa thinks. But walking backwards doesn't work out so well for Theresa.

Manny is still dancing. He spins into Theresa's path just as she approaches. He drops low, and not having eyes in the back of her head, Theresa doesn't notice that they are about to collide. She trips over Manny, landing hard on her rear. *Couldn't have happened to a nicer person*, Rosa thinks.

Manny seemed slightly more sympathetic. He pulls her up, apologizing profusely. The back of Theresa's pants is soaked with mud. In the usually dry field, she has found a rare wet spot. Rosa laughs to herself. But she doesn't dwell on Theresa.

Kyle is still walking toward her. She locks eyes with him and loses sight of everything and everyone else around her. She tries to play it cool, but she can't. Rosa's face breaks into a wide smile, mirroring the expression worn by Kyle Baron.

Finally, he stands before her, only inches away. He leans in close, trying to speak over Terrance's blaring stereo. "I didn't think you'd come! What a nice surprise!"

Rosa is suddenly warm. She looks down at the ground, realizing the toe of her white sneaker is damp and stained with mud. She'll have to clean that before her mother sees. She shakes thoughts of her mother from her head and returns to the present moment.

Suddenly, the song comes to an end, and the night air softens. Voices murmur, people chill. And then Terrance yells, "Time for a slow song!"

Kyle raises his eyebrows and holds out his hands. And for about two and a half glorious minutes, Rosa's world is perfect. She isn't thinking about her missing father. She isn't racked with guilt about lying to her mother. She is swaying in the arms of Kyle Baron, and for this brief, magnificent moment, everything feels right. Perhaps for the last time in her life.

Because as the song ends, in that flash of a moment before another song begins, Kyle releases Rosa. He takes a step back. And then Rick Santini yells, "Kyle, go long!" The crowd erupts in cheers as Rick pulls the ball back over his shoulder. At first, it's a pump fake. But Kyle laughs and runs toward the shroud of fog that hangs as a backdrop.

Rick Santini launches the ball. It soars through the air, the music begins pumping again, and Kyle disappears into the fog. The cheering continues. The music continues. The dancing continues. And then it all stops. And they wait. And wait. They call his name into the mist. But Kyle Baron does not return.

5

"Mama, *please!*" Rosa pleads. "I told you, I was only supposed to be there a little while. Everyone was going. What was I supposed to do?!"

Marisol Vieja stops pacing and looks at Rosa with red, swollen eyes. Rosary beads dangle from her hand, and her voice trembles. "I warned you. There was a full moon. You know what happened the last time there was a full moon." She takes a deep breath and steadies her voice. "But against my better judgment, I let you go to the game, and—"

"And when you gave me an inch, I took a mile. You've said this already!" Rosa not only interrupts her mother but raises her voice. And she immediately regrets it.

A fire burns behind Marisol's eyes. "Do not speak to me in that tone. You are my life, Rosa. You are all I have left. What I do . . ." Her words turn into sobs. Her shoulders sink, her hard edge softens, and she murmurs prayers while clutching the rosary.

Rosa softens as well. "I'm sorry," she says. "It was foolish. I thought we would just go to the party for a little while, and then Manny would bring me home while you were still at work. But then the police were called, and we had to stay there for questioning, and I was the last one to speak to Kyle before—" Now Rosa breaks down in sobs.

"Shhh," Marisol coaxes. She puts a hand on Rosa's head and pulls it to her shoulder. "My baby, I know. I know." A long moment of tender silence passes between them. And in that moment, they both relive that night a month before. That night when Luca did not come home. That night when the deputies exchanged nervous glances and asked if there had been any indication that he might be planning to leave.

Marisol puts her hands on Rosa's shoulders and pushes her back, holding on until her fragile daughter is able to once again stand on her own. She looks directly into Rosa's deep brown eyes and asks, "And now, today, why do you want to go to that field and live this nightmare all over again?"

Rosa takes a deep breath. "Mama, it's a search party. People from all over Foggy Creek will be there. And they need a lot of people. We'll cover a large area. We'll search for Kyle. And maybe . . ." Her voice trails off. She is unable to form the words. But Marisol understands. Maybe they will find something that explains why Luca never returned a month ago.

Marisol drops her arms to her sides and nods. "Okay. I give my permission. You may join the search party today."

Rosa throws her arms around her mother's

shoulders. "Mama, thank you. I promise I will come straight home after the search."

Marisol backs away so that she can look Rosa in the eyes again. "Yes, you will. And you will call me from this house when you are safely back inside."

"Yes, Mama," Rosa eagerly concedes.

"And after that, you will stay here."

"Yes, Mama."

"And this doesn't change the fact that you are grounded for the next two weeks."

Rosa nods her understanding, and mother and daughter hug once more.

Manny's car bumps along the familiar rutted road. They follow a long line of vehicles until they reach a sheriff's deputy in a bright yellow vest. He directs them toward an area roped off for parking, and Manny files in. He and Rosa walk in silent lockstep to join the gathering.

Rosa tries to make a quick estimate. There must be at least five hundred people. All there to search for Kyle Baron.

Theresa Colon sobs into a tissue. Her eyes are red, but her hair and make-up are perfect, as usual. Theresa's posse clings to her sides. The girls take turns patting her back, hugging her, both providing and attracting attention.

Rick Santini, pale and hollow-eyed, stands with the rest of the football team. They all wear Foggy Creek High jerseys and have tied shreds of white T-shirts around their biceps as makeshift armbands. On the armbands, with black permanent markers, they've printed his name, KYLE.

There's an ambulance with paramedics on hand. The local Chamber of Commerce has assembled volunteers from all over the county, each wearing a shirt or hat emblazoned with the name of their respective business.

The searchers gather in front of a hastily erected information stage. The sheriff holds a battery-powered megaphone. He taps a button, and a high-pitched screech demands attention. Next, his amplified voice details the search procedure and sorts the volunteers into two long lines, spread wide across the expanse of the field.

Manny and Rosa are assigned to the second line, searching behind the first to make sure nothing is missed. Another electronic screech blares, and both lines begin to inch forward, eyes glued to the ground for any clue, any shred of evidence that Kyle had existed here only hours before. That somehow, he might still exist.

Despite the day's heat, a chill runs down Rosa's spine. If she hadn't been there, Kyle would not have been standing where he was, talking to her. Perhaps the ball would have been thrown in a different direction. Or maybe it wouldn't have been thrown at all. Rosa shakes away the thoughts and continues walking in silence.

Suddenly, voices shout. The electronic screech blares again. It's followed by the sheriff's voice, loud and distorted, through a megaphone. "Stop where you are! Do not advance! Please return to the information stage immediately." The words are repeated again and again as the searchers turn and huddle in groups, murmuring and speculating.

Rosa walks with Manny and decides to unload some of her private thoughts. "You know, there was a full moon last night, right?"

"I guess so," Manny answers. "I wasn't really focused on the sky."

"And the last time there was a full moon, it was the night my father disappeared." She lets those words hang there, giving Manny space to process the connection.

The sheriff makes his way to the stage, megaphone in hand. He gives them the news. A sinkhole has been discovered. Everyone is directed to vacate the premises in a quick but orderly fashion.

As they walk to Manny's car along with the swarm of concerned but slightly frightened searchers, Rosa resumes her earlier conversation. "Anyway, the full moon. Don't you think it's strange?"

"I guess," Manny responds. "I mean, the moon has something to do with tides, but do you think it has anything to do with sinkholes? I need to pay better attention in science."

"I'm not talking about science," Rosa replies. She hesitates, but then she decides to confide in Manny about the voice. "There's something else. Thursday night, I couldn't sleep. I was sitting on the side of my bed. The window was open."

Manny's forehead wrinkles, and she knows she has created an awkward vibe. But she decides to finish. She needs to finish.

"And then there was a voice."

"Okay, hold on." Manny says. "Are you saying someone was outside your house?"

"No," Rosa continues. "It wasn't coming from my yard. It came from the east, from the fog, from somewhere out here."

Manny nods cautiously and looks at Rosa with concern. "What did this voice say?" he asks quietly.

Rosa takes a deep breath. "It said 'innocent blood.'"

They reach the car, and Manny turns to Rosa. In his face, she sees a mix of compassion and concern. And then his words follow, "Look, Rosa, you've been through a lot lately. It's understandable. Your mind is playing tricks on you."

"Never mind," she hastily replies, instantly regretting that she has said anything at all. She climbs into the car, determined to change the subject and hoping Manny will forget what she's told him.

What she fails to notice is that Theresa Colon is parked next to them. She sits in the driver's seat with her window rolled down, and she has just heard every word that Rosa said.

By Saturday evening, Dawson County's
sinkhole is a breaking story all over the state.
Rosa watches it all on the six o'clock news
while eating a bowl of reheated chicken
soup. Her mother is working the late shift
at the diner again, but this time Rosa isn't
going anywhere.

The camera pans across the old oil
field, and it is alive with activity. A team
of geophysicists from Southern Methodist
University had set up equipment around
the sinkhole. Yellow caution tape outlines

their work area. Outside the yellow boundary, reporters, cameras, microphones, and vans topped with satellite dishes all compete for attention.

Suddenly, Kyle Baron's photo is on the screen. Rosa's heart drops, and she puts her soup bowl down on the coffee table. Kyle's green eyes, his sandy hair, his kind smile— they look so real, so close. Like he is standing in front of her.

The station cuts back to the newsroom. A small picture of Rosa's father floats next to the anchor's head. Her expression suddenly somber, she says, "Local surveyor Luca Vieja disappeared about a month ago." Rosa freezes. Involuntary tears pour onto her cheeks. "Authorities now speculate that he may have been the first victim of the sinkhole. However, if you have any information as to his whereabouts, please call the sheriff's tip line." A phone number appears at the bottom of the screen. And then it all disappears. The anchor flashes her characteristic smile. "Now in other news . . ."

Rosa grabs the remote and turns off the television. She leans back on the couch and wipes the tears from her face. *Maybe*, she thinks, *Manny is right. I've been through a lot. I need to get a grip.*

Suddenly, as if her thoughts have summoned him, Manny sends a text. Rosa lifts her phone from the coffee table and reads:

> What are you doing? Can you talk?

Curious, she calls immediately. "Manny," she says, "I saw the news. I know they said that maybe my dad—"

"It's not that," Manny interrupts. "There's something else you need to know." He spills his words out quickly at first and then stops. And she waits.

Finally, Rosa says, "Okay, what is it?" The tears are gone now, replaced by worry.

"Yesterday, when you told me about hearing a voice," Manny begins.

"Yeah, about that," she says.

"No, listen," Manny continues. "I didn't notice, but Theresa must have been close enough to hear."

A tremor runs through Rosa's entire body. "Manny," she says, "what is she doing?"

"She's telling everybody about the voice, but she's making it sound like you're communicating with evil spirits or something."

"What?! That's ridiculous!" Rosa's worry dissipates, replaced by anger. "She has some nerve!"

"I'm not finished. She's making it sound like you somehow conjured the sinkhole. That you were desperate to keep Kyle away from her, and you—"

"You've got to be kidding! Who would believe something so ridiculous?"

Manny is silent for a moment. Then he says, "You might want to check social media."

Rosa ends the call quickly, fueled by anger and disbelief. But Manny is right. As she scrolls through social media, post after post reduces her until she no longer feels the anger. Just shock. And fear. And disbelief. *Rosa the Witch*.

Sorceress of Foggy Creek. Beware the wrath of Rosa Vieja. Pictures of her have been altered in various ways. Rosa in a black hat and cape. Rosa with green skin. Rosa with lightning bolts extending from her fingertips.

But the comments are worse than the pictures.

You must admit, there's something strange about that girl.

I always feel a cold chill when she walks by.

It's the quiet ones you should fear.

Man, what did her dad do to make her eliminate him?

Rosa throws the phone on the couch and screams. And there, alone in her home, she grabs the sides of her head and squeezes. She tries to force the feelings to escape through loud, guttural sounds. She moans, she wails, she cries. But no matter what she does to force the feelings out of her, they remain.

Moving mechanically, she dumps the soup and washes her bowl. She straightens the pillows on the sofa and carries the phone to her bedside table. And then she takes the hottest shower she could endure. She tries to wash the words away like dirt. Like mud. Like germs. And then she pulls the headphones from her desk drawer and wraps them around her head like some form of protection. A safety helmet. Something to block out the world and the voices.

Rosa opens a playlist on her phone. She crawls into bed and curls into a fetal position. Shielded from voices, she keeps her back to the window and closes her eyes, so she won't see her father's face staring back at her from behind glass. And once she feels completely safe from the world, Rosa finally sleeps.

Her first plan is to fake an illness. Smear a tiny bit of mascara beneath her eyes. Wrap herself in a blanket and pretend to be cold. Cough a few times. But she can't lie to her mother again. Not now.

So, Rosa gathers her books and packs her lunch. She eats her breakfast and tries to make pleasant conversation with her mom. As she walks to the bus stop, she tries to breathe in peace and breathe out the anxiety. Something she heard from a self-help podcast. It isn't working.

The other people at her bus stop huddle together, and Rosa stands alone. But that's not unusual. She can't hear their conversation, but she sees the occasional glances in her direction. She suddenly wishes she had brought a book. Not a textbook, but some paperback where she could bury her nose and completely ignore them. For now, she tries to appear unusually fascinated by her ability to move rocks with the toe of her shoe.

Once she's on the bus, the others aren't so guarded. From somewhere behind her, Rosa hears a pathetic attempt at what she guesses is supposed to be a ghost sound. *Woooooooo!*

She turns toward the sound, her anxiety morphing into irritation. There are giggles and squirms. A couple of kids seemed intensely interested in the contents of their backpacks. Some sink down in their seats, as if hiding from her eyes.

At school, things are no better. Whispers. Glances. Heads that quickly turn away when she looks in their direction. Rosa stares into her locker, but her mind relives the comments:

You must admit, there's something strange about that girl.
I always feel a cold chill when she walks by.
It's the quiet ones you should fear.
Man, what did her dad do to make her eliminate him?

She fights back tears. She swallows hard. *Breathe in the peace. Breathe out the anxiety.*

"Something very serious must be going on inside your locker." Manny's voice startles her. She jumps. So much for breathing out the anxiety.

"Manny, you were right. How can so many people suddenly jump on board with Theresa's crazy story?" She stares at Manny, knowing his eyes are the only ones she will be able to look directly into until this whole thing blows over. If this whole thing blows over.

Manny is serious. Not his typical approach. "I'm sorry, Rosa," he begins. "Look, you were the one who brought the whole thing up. You were the one who mentioned the creepy voice. You were the one who mentioned blood."

A flash of anger seizes Rosa. She whisper-yells, trying to contain her rage. "I was sharing something privately with a friend I thought I could trust."

"Hold on," he shoots back. "I'm not criticizing. I'm not the bad guy here." Manny closes his locker, secures the lock, and turns the combination three times. "I'm just saying, you *did* mention those things. What Theresa is doing with it is wrong. What everybody's saying is crazy. But you have to admit, it kind of all started with you."

Suddenly Rosa's anger is replaced by self-doubt. By self-hate. By regret. She wishes she had never mentioned the voice. *Breathe in the peace. Breathe out the anxiety.* If only this practice actually worked.

"Come on," Manny says. "We're going to be late to history if we don't hurry. Mr. White said our tests are graded. Now, that's something to look forward to," he quips. And then he smiles. Rosa closes her locker, telling herself that maybe things will continue to inch a little closer to normal as the day goes on. Maybe.

Rosa takes her seat in the front of the class just as the bell rings. Usually, she likes sitting up front. It's easier for her to pay attention. To block out distractions. But suddenly, sitting up front feels like being on stage. All eyes, all attention, all interest seems focused on her.

She tries to ignore the whispers. At first, she resists the temptation to turn around. *But maybe*, she thinks, *maybe it's not about me. Maybe I'm being hypersensitive.* So, she attempts a casual glance. And immediately, heads turn, eyes are averted. From the back of the room, someone yells, "Don't hurt me!" And the class erupts in laughter.

Rosa's eyes find Manny. He is the one person not laughing. He sits with his back against the side wall and offers a slight shake of his head. A sympathetic half-smile. A shrug.

Suddenly, Mr. White throws a textbook down onto his wooden desk, and the room is silenced. "I wasn't sure what I was going to have to do to get your attention," he says. His thin frame and pale skin usually made him the least intimidating teacher on campus. Of course, he hasn't been at Foggy Creek High long enough for anybody to really know what he's capable of. There is a fury in his eyes and a chill in his voice. Maybe he's a force to be reckoned with after all.

The room is silent. Very quietly, Mr. White continues. "Obviously, you are not as eager to receive your test grades as I had thought." A groan sweeps across the room, and Rosa feels a small wave of relief that attention and reactions have moved to something other than her.

"Enough," he says. Mr. White runs a hand through his brown hair, pushing it away from his face in exasperation. "Your tests are here." He points to the corner of his desk. "You can pick them up on your way out of class. For now, we move on to World War I."

Mr. White launches into a story about the assassination of Franz Ferdinand, the archduke of Austria. Rosa tries to become absorbed in note taking, but it's impossible to ignore the whispers.

Suddenly, Mr. White moves his lecture away from the whiteboard and walks toward his students. He stops just past Rosa's desk, and she can no longer see his face. However, she hears his voice very clearly.

"You may think that stories from the past are not interesting. You may think they have nothing to do with your lives today." The whispers have stopped, mainly because of his proximity. "However, you must pay attention to the stories of the past. Especially the stories that involve an unjust death," he says. "Because there is always a reckoning when innocent blood is shed."

The bell rings, but Rosa remains in her seat, paralyzed by his words. Student after student files past. They pick up their tests and move along. Finally, Rosa approaches his desk. She retrieves her test paper and he says, "Good job, Rosa. I know that studying must have been hard, under the circumstances. I'm sorry about your dad."

There are no tears at the mention of her father. There is no eagerness to check her grade. Instead, Rosa's mind is focused on one thing only. "Mr. White, you talked about a reckoning, about innocent blood." She stares into his gray eyes and once again feels a chill. "Can I speak to you about it after school?"

After her last class, Rosa strolls slowly to her locker. Usually, she's in a rush to make sure she has everything she needs for homework and studying before dashing out to the bus ramp. She pulls her phone from her backpack and sends a quick text to her mom.

> FYI - Going to be late. Staying after school for a study session with my history teacher. Will walk home after

She has failed to notice Manny standing right next to her. "Do you need a ride? I think I hear the buses pulling out."

"No, thanks," Rosa replies. "I arranged to talk with Mr. White after school. I'll just walk home after."

"Test grade that bad?" Manny asks.

Her immediate desire is to tell him about her 96 percent on the history test. However, she doesn't want to have to explain her actual purpose. So, she settles for saying, "Yeah, something like that."

"Okay, well," Manny looks at the speckled tile floor while Rosa scans the hall. The school is beginning to clear. The looks, the comments, the whispers are fading away. "So, you'll be okay?" he asks.

"Yeah, I'll be fine," she tells him. "Some fresh air and exercise will be good for me."

Manny laughs. "It'll probably take like an hour to walk home from here. You want me to wait and give you a ride?"

"No," she says, "I'm in the mood for a walk."

Manny shrugs, and after three turns of his combination lock and one of his characteristic half-smiles, he turns and leaves.

Rosa walks into Mr. White's room and takes a seat at her usual desk. It's only a moment before her teacher appears. "Rosa, I'm glad you're here!" he says. "Sorry to keep you waiting. I had bus duty today." He sits in the stiff wooden chair behind his desk and lets out a sigh. "Now, what was it you wanted to talk about?"

"Today, in class, when you were talking about the assassination of Franz Ferdinand, you said there is always a reckoning when innocent blood is shed." Rosa pauses, hoping he will start talking. But he only stares at her, his gray eyes eerily hypnotic. She clears her throat and continues. "It just didn't seem like you were talking about World War I. I was just wondering . . ."

This time he completes her sentence. "You were wondering if there is another story on my mind?"

"Yeah, I guess so. I mean, something about those words seemed familiar, so I was just curious." This situation is foreign and awkward. Initiating conversation is neither natural nor comfortable for her. Usually she listens, she contemplates, she responds. At this point, she desperately hopes Mr. White will take over the conversation. And then he does.

"You're very perceptive," he tells her. "There *is* a story I was thinking about, and it has nothing to do with World War I." He leans forward, resting his elbows on the desk. "No, I was thinking about a piece of local lore. The legend of Bucky LeBlanc."

Rosa fights the urge to laugh. Is he making this up? Is he trying to lighten the mood and ease her tension? Then the self-doubt returns. Is he actually ridiculing her? Making up something ridiculous to belittle her fears? Her internal struggle is quickly pushed aside as Mr. White begins to recount the legend.

"The year was 1894," he begins. "Bucky LeBlanc was a wide-eyed dreamer from the swamps of Louisiana. He was tired of bugs, bayous, and black water. One day, Bucky read an ad about cheap land being sold to settlers who were willing to work with the dry ground and near-desert climate of Foggy Creek, Texas. And Bucky thought he'd found his ticket to a new life.

"So, Bucky loaded up what little he had and headed west. He spent every cent he had to buy 85 acres from a man named Horatio Baron. You see, ol' Horatio had purchased the land years before on speculation that the railroad would come right through the middle of it. He stood to make a fortune with hotels, saloons, restaurants, and the like.

"However, plans changed, and the railroad got routed somewhere else. Horatio Baron was stuck with worthless land and wanted to unload it. So, he put it up for sale. And our young dreamer, Bucky LeBlanc, was happy to buy it. Bucky dreamed of being a cattle rancher. Of course, before any other parts of his dream could materialize, he was going to need water. So, Bucky began to dig a well.

"Imagine Bucky's disappointment when he

hit upon black liquid. He felt like he was right back in the swamps of Louisiana. Right back in the bayou he worked so hard to escape. So, Bucky went to see Horatio Baron. He told him about the black water. He said he didn't realize he'd bought swampland, and he wanted to know what Mr. Baron planned to do to make it right.

"Well, that's where Bucky's story ends. He was never seen or heard from again. Horatio Baron reclaimed the land and destroyed any evidence that Bucky LeBlanc had ever purchased the property. You see, Baron knew that the black water Bucky had discovered was oil. And being a greedy and unscrupulous man, he decided not to tell Bucky about the oil and its value. Instead, he just decided to get rid of Bucky and reclaim the land.

"Now, a lot of people say this is just a story. They claim Bucky LeBlanc never existed. But others feel quite certain that Baron took advantage of the poor, naive lad. They think he killed Bucky, buried him somewhere on that property, and went on to enjoy all the wealth that oil brought to him. And all the while, he pretended that Bucky LeBlanc never existed."

Mr. White took a deep breath and leaned against the back of his chair. "So, there you have it."

"But the part about the reckoning?" Rosa asks.

"If indeed Horatio Baron killed Bucky LeBlanc and made his fortune from what rightfully belonged to Bucky, that was wrong. And wrongs just don't lie down and go to sleep. Bucky's murder, that was innocent blood. And now, the reckoning has come."

Rosa sits quietly, trying to process the meaning of this legend that may or may not be true. But suddenly, she's hit with a disturbing thought. *Horatio Baron. Kyle Baron. Is there a connection? Was Kyle a descendent of the man who supposedly committed this terrible wrong?*

She looks up in distress but is unable to speak. Mr. White's gray eyes seem to swirl like storm clouds. "Th-thank you," Rosa says.

"Um, I need to be going. My mom expects me home." She quickly gathers her things and leaves the room. And as she passes through the classroom door, a chill creeps down her spine.

Over the course of her long walk home, Rosa is lost in thought. A local legend. It seems so silly. She doesn't know a lot of local history, but she knows Foggy Creek's abandoned oil field has been a desolate space for decades. She has no idea who owns it.

And Kyle Baron. Could he have been related to Horatio Baron? Was Mr. White trying to tell her that Kyle's death was in some way paying for the sins of an ancestor? How does Mr. White know all of this? It's not like he's a local. He only started teaching at Foggy

Creek High recently, and no one knows much about him.

Rosa shudders remembering the motion she saw in his steely gray eyes. Or did she really see it? First hearing voices, now seeing Mr. White's eyes swirling. Maybe Manny is right. She's been through a lot lately.

When her father first disappeared, Rosa held onto hope. She was sure he would return. There would be an explanation. Maybe he was lying in a ditch somewhere, injured. Some Good Samaritan would find him and take him to a hospital. There would be a phone call. Tears of relief and joy. The waiting would end, and everything would go back to normal.

But as time passed, hopes for finding Luca diminished. The rumors began. But Rosa knows they can't be true. Her family is tight. Her father had plans for their future. There's no way he would leave. However, as twisted as it seems, Rosa still clings to those rumors. If he chose to leave them, that means he's still out there somewhere. And if he's still out there somewhere, that means he could still come back.

By the time Rosa gets home, her water bottle is empty, and her head is filled with confusion. All the thinking has not allowed her to sort things out. It has caused her to relive the pain. She is happy to fall into her mother's waiting arms. But why is her mother home from Rose Grocery? And why is she sobbing?

"Mama, what is it?" Rosa asks.

Marisol Vieja takes a deep breath, closes her eyes, and makes the sign of the cross. She leads Rosa to the sofa, and they sit facing each other. Then her mother begins to speak. "The sheriff called," she says. "They have found your father's truck."

As her mother struggles to remain calm and continue speaking, Rosa fights to breathe. It's as if she's been punched in the gut. She knows that nothing good can follow this news. She holds tightly to her mother's trembling hands and listens as the next words come.

"His truck was parked off the road in a thicket of bushes and trees. He found some shade to keep the truck from getting too hot, but . . ." she dissolves into tears, so Rosa finishes the sentence for her.

"So that's why they didn't find the truck when they searched. But Mama, how did they find it now?" She is breathing again, thinking logically, trying to be the strong one now.

"It's the people who are studying the sinkhole. They found it." Marisol wipes tears from her face. "They feel certain that your father was the first victim of the sinkhole. They feel certain he's gone."

Mother and daughter cling to one another in a mix of mourning and relief. No more searching. No more wondering. And yet, he is gone. Luca Vieja is truly gone, and the two of them are alone.

Soon their mourning turns to reminiscing. They recall the way he made them laugh. They smile remembering the pure joy he found in something as simple as pizza and ice cream. They recall the way he loved. And they recall the way he dreamed. Because Luca Vieja had certainly been a dreamer.

Finally, Marisol stands and says, "I need to get ready. My shift at the diner starts soon."

"Mama, you're not going!" Rosa protests. "You can't go in this state. After this news. Surely, they will understand."

Marisol raises a steady hand to silence her daughter. "There is no one available to work for me tonight. I checked. I've already lost hours from the grocery because I left early." She wraps Rosa in a warm hug and then pulls back to look her in the eyes. "Work will keep my mind busy. It's you I worry about."

"I have work, too," Rosa assures her. "I will stay busy." But internally, she longs for her mother's company. She needs a steady heartbeat near her own. She dreads the moment when darkness falls, and the house becomes silent.

"Good," Marisol says. "And when you're hungry, there's a special treat." Although tears still well in her eyes, a warm grin spreads across her face. "Pizza and ice cream."

Rosa watches the evening news and sees images of her father's truck. She searches for something else to watch, something to read, something to do to keep her mind from exploding, to silence the breaking of her heart.

She knows better than to go on social media. She can't fall into Theresa's trap. She puts her phone on Do Not Disturb mode and turns it face down on her bedside table. Exhausted from the emotions, from the long walk, from Mr. White's puzzling words, she is sure that sleep will come easily. And it does come for a while. But then she is awake, staring at the moonlight that outlines the edges of her window shade.

Rosa tosses and turns, unable to silence the voices echoing in her head. *Tonight, we feast. Pizza and ice cream. They found his truck. He's gone. There's always a reckoning. Innocent blood.* Rosa sits up and turns on the lamp. She wants to know the time but resists the urge to look at her phone.

She walks into the kitchen to check the digital clock on the microwave. It's 1:15 a.m. She gets a glass of water and tiptoes to her mother's room. She gently opens the door, just enough to see that Marisol is sleeping, no doubt completely exhausted. She closes the door and creeps back to her room.

She raises the shade on her window and stares out into the night. The landscape is only a collection of shadows at night. Above it all, a million tiny spots of starlight pierce the sky the way memories pierce her heart. And there, standing alone, fully awake, Rosa hears the voice again. *Innocent blood.*

"Rosa, you should be awake." Marisol Vieja sits on the edge of the bed rubbing her daughter's back and coaxing her into consciousness.

Rosa rolls to her side. She squints in resistance to bright sunlight streaming through the open window. She studies her mother's calm but somber face. And then she lifts her phone to see that it is already 7:15. She has only twenty minutes to get to the bus stop.

"It's okay," her mother tells her, reading her panicked expression. "I will drive you to school. But let's get you moving, okay?" A kiss on the forehead, a pat on the shoulder, and then she is leaving the room. "I'll put together a breakfast you can eat in the car," she calls back over her shoulder.

Rosa nods and sits up. Thoughts of the previous day rush into her waking mind. Thoughts of Theresa's cruel rumors spreading like wildfire. Thoughts of Mr. White, Bucky LeBlanc, the truck, the news. And thoughts of the voice she heard in the middle of the night.

A dream. She tells herself. *It was just a dream.* With a deep breath and hope for a fresh start, Rosa dresses and gathers her things. Before leaving, she lowers the shade on her window, and a chilling thought paralyzes her. The shade is up. On the bedside table is a half-empty glass of water.

"Rosa! Let's go!" Her mother's voice is more urgent now. There's no time to think, no time to process. *You've been through a lot lately.* Manny's voice echoes in her mind, far more comforting than the voice she heard only hours ago. Rosa shakes her head, as if she can rid it of the thoughts that threaten to open the earth beneath her and drag her down.

Soon she is in the car, washing a scrambled egg sandwich down with a tiny can of pineapple juice. "I've taken the morning off because I have to go to the sheriff's office and complete some paperwork," Marisol says tenderly, even though her daughter has not thought to ask for an explanation. "But I will stay late at the grocery and won't have time to come home before my shift at the diner. You'll be okay?"

Rosa nods. "I'll be fine."

Marisol smiles weakly. "There's leftover pizza," she offers.

The first bell rings as Rosa exits the car, and she must rush to first period to make it before the tardy bell. That eliminates time in the hall and time at her locker. And that's okay. She can avoid the stares and the whispers, and besides, she has everything she needs in her backpack.

But deep inside, there is an ache because

she isn't starting her day with Manny's smile, his enthusiasm, the three turns of his combination lock. As she falls into her front-row seat, she glances to the side wall and catches his eyes. There is no reassuring smile, but his head nods slightly. An acknowledgement, at least.

As Mr. White continues his World War I lecture, Rosa struggles to concentrate and take notes. But something within her is fighting back with unrelenting resistance. Her hand trembles uncontrollably, making it difficult to write. Her mind sees images, hears voices. It was an unwelcome intrusion but one she has no ability to ignore.

"Rosa, are you okay?" Mr. White stands by her desk. His voice is gentle, and he waits for a response. During the moments of silence, the whispers began. A couple of giggles. A fake cough.

Just before Rosa can answer, another fake cough, this time spitting out the word, "Sorceress." The class erupts in laughter.

"Silence!" Mr. White's gray eyes turn to

charcoal. There's a fury in his tone that brings the laughter to an abrupt end. And then the bell rings, bringing first period to an abrupt end as well.

Rosa silently collects her things. There are no tears to suppress. She has emptied herself of tears. But as she edges around Mr. White, who still hovers near her desk, he speaks once more. "It's not your fault. I'm sorry."

She looks back at him and sees that his gray eyes hold no fury. "I'm so sorry," he says once more, and Rosa leaves the room.

After that, something changes. There are no more whispers and giggles. No more fake coughs and labels. Instead, people distance themselves from Rosa in a whole new way. When she walks down the hall, the crowd parts, creating an open path for her. Creating a barrier of space for themselves.

When she sits in a class, the only sound she hears is the ear-splitting scrape of desks being dragged across the tile floor as classmates try to mask their efforts to move inches farther away from her. The whole world seems to be pulling itself back and creating a vacuum in which Rosa suddenly finds herself.

At lunch time, she is relieved to find Manny sitting alone at their usual outdoor table. Finally, someone to connect with, to talk to. Rosa drops her backpack on the table and drops herself onto the bench across from him.

Manny looks around, conscious of the stares, and Rosa suddenly feels like an alien in her own skin. "You too?" she asks Manny.

She begins to gather her things, but he says, "No, wait." His face softens, and he attempts a smile. "Please, sit with me."

Rosa sinks back onto the bench. Her expression is blank. She feels nothing but exhaustion. "Manny, you and my mom are the only ones left."

"I know," he says. "And I'm sorry. I didn't know if you'd be here today after they found . . ." he paused. "You know . . ."

Of course, she knows. They found the truck. They know her father didn't leave.

He's gone, but he's a victim. No different from Kyle Baron. "Thanks." It's all she could manage to say.

They eat in silence until Manny finally asks, "So how are you?"

Her first instinct is to leave it at *I'm fine*, but she can't do that. She needs to talk, and there is no one else who will listen. So, she decides to tell him.

"Manny, remember when Mr. White said, 'There's always a reckoning when innocent blood is shed?'" Manny nods passively, so she continues. "Innocent blood, those words. I was curious so I talked to him after school." She goes on to tell Manny about the legend of Bucky LeBlanc, and ends with, "So what if maybe the sinkhole is the reckoning? What if Kyle Baron is a descendent of Horatio Baron, and—"

"Rosa! You're not making things any easier on yourself!" Manny's words are sharp, and he's breathing deeply. "Listen, sinkholes aren't some kind of paranormal occurrence. Have you been watching the news? They have geophysicists explaining this stuff. The ground was unstable after years of drilling. It's science. Don't turn it into superstition."

Rosa feels like she's been slapped in the face. The questions that plague her have been dismissed so easily. But Manny. He's the only one left. So, in desperation, she goes ahead and spills the rest. "Manny, I heard the voice again. *Innocent blood.* And I know it wasn't a dream." She presents her evidence—the raised shade, the half-empty glass of water on her bedside table—but listening to her own voice, she realizes how ridiculous it sounds.

The bell rings, and Manny quickly gathers his things. Before leaving her alone, he turns back and says, "Rosa, look. Why don't you just give it all a rest for now. At least until the rumors die down."

She wants to plead for her one friend to remain on her side, but before she can find the words, he speaks with finality. "Just let it go, okay?" And Manny walks away.

As Manny walks away, Rosa watches her last connection to the outside world dissolve.
For the first time in her life, she feels truly alone. She walks to class in the vacuum that is becoming familiar. She searches faces for some indication of recognition, of acknowledgement. But it's as if she doesn't exist. And this, she realizes, is her new reality.

By the end of the day, it's as if she's walking under water. The other faces are a blur. Their sounds are muffled and indistinguishable. She moves slowly, pushing gently against the pressure. No mad dash to her locker alongside Manny's. No desire to force herself into a bus where others consciously avoid her.

Rosa decides to make the long walk home again. Her mother won't be home until after midnight. There is no need to rush in her underwater world.

She drifts past Mr. White's room, where he sits at his desk. After a few steps, she stops, feeling drawn to his open door. Perhaps she is not completely alone. At least there is Mr. White to talk to. Maybe she can confide in him about the voice. Maybe he can make sense of it, counsel her, offer wisdom. And so, she turns and retraces her steps. She stands in the doorway and knocks softly, not wanting to startle him.

"Rosa," he says. He looks at his watch, and her immediate impulse is to run, but again, she senses the pressure all around her, and movement is difficult. Running is not possible "I'm just tying up some loose ends. Do you need to discuss something?"

Yes, Rosa thinks. *I need to discuss something,*

but do I dare? Will I drive you away too? Am I really some kind of freak, and should I reveal that to anyone else? A million thoughts swim through her mind, but her voice says only, "Yes, if you have a minute."

He stands but remains behind his desk. He smiles. He waves a hand to usher her to her seat in the front of the room. And she follows his silent guidance. "What's going on?" he asks.

"It's not about what we're studying in class," she begins, just to be clear. "It's the legend."

He nods and says, "Yes, I didn't think we were finished discussing this."

"I've given it a lot of thought," Rosa says. "Bucky was naive and innocent."

"Yes, he was quite a young dreamer," Mr. White adds wistfully, as if reminiscing about an old friend. "He was not wise to the ways of the world, and it cost him his life."

"But that shouldn't have happened," Rosa says. "It was wrong. What Horatio Baron did— if the story is correct—was wrong. Bucky should not have died."

"No," Mr. White concedes. And then he leans forward, consumed by a new intensity. "Bucky LeBlanc should have become a very rich man. The land rightfully belonged to him. That oil could have been the key to unlocking his dreams, and he had his whole life ahead of him."

The gray of his eyes once again swirl like storm clouds. Rosa feels like she's struggling against two opposing currents. One tries to pull her away from this story that is becoming too real; from this man who speaks of it with such passion. The other seeks to lure her in a new direction, one that is misty and undefined. But Rosa is anchored by her need to share this secret with someone because the burden is too great for her to bear alone. And so, she stays.

"You said something about a reckoning," she says. "I realize that the innocent blood was Bucky's, but what do you mean by a reckoning?"

Mr. White's eyes grow dark now, and he leans against the straight back of his wooden chair. "A reckoning," he begins, "means it's time to deal with something—or someone

—you have ignored for too long." He sits in silence, staring past Rosa, beyond the walls of the classroom, fixated on something she cannot see.

"And so, this sinkhole . . ." Rosa swallows. She wants him to finish the sentence for her, but he seems to have been transported somewhere else. She clears her throat and continues. "This sinkhole might be a reckoning of some sort? It might be Bucky LeBlanc's way of finally getting some kind of recognition? Or maybe some type of revenge?"

Still staring past her, he answers. "Yes, it could be that." He takes a deep breath, and his gaze returns to Rosa. "So, do you think that's crazy?" He smiles.

Rosa feels a sense of relief, as if he has opened the door for her to tell him about the voice. Maybe he won't think she has imagined it. Maybe he will understand. And so, she sets aside her fears and opens up to him.

"I've heard this voice," she says. "It comes from somewhere east of my house, where the wilderness begins. I think it might be coming from the abandoned oil field."

His gaze is steady. No judgment. No sudden concern. "And what does this voice say?" he asks.

Rosa swallows hard and says, "Innocent blood."

Mr. White smiles. In all her calculations, she has not predicted this reaction. "You don't think I'm crazy?" she asks.

"No," Mr. White replies. "I think you have a gift. You have a special connection to the spirit world. You should nurture your gift, no matter what others think."

As he speaks, the storm clouds are once again set in motion, and so is the current that pulls her away. Suddenly, she can think of nothing she wants more than to be out of his presence. Out of this classroom. Away from the school. A cold chill runs down her spine.

"Thank you," she says. "I guess that's it." Rosa hurriedly gathers her things. Her heart races, and she takes only quick, shallow breaths. It is only when she is outside the doors of the school that she allows herself to pause, to breathe normally, to calm her heart. But despite the warmth of the day and the unrelenting sunshine, she cannot escape the chill.

As Rosa approaches her house, warm from the sun and physically exhausted, she is met with a surprise. A shiny white SUV is parked in the driveway. A woman jumps from the driver's seat and waves to her.

The woman wears black yoga pants and a long pink shirt that says, "Messy hair, don't care!" It's ironic, Rosa thinks. Not a single brown hair on her head is out of place. The woman raises a manicured hand to shield her eyes, and as Rosa cautiously approaches, the passenger door begins to open.

Out steps Theresa Colon, hands clasped in front of her and innocent pout on her face. "Hi, Rosa," Theresa says. She lifts a hand in the direction of the woman and adds, "This is my mom."

The woman takes the cue and reveals their mission. "We are so sorry about your father. You must be heartbroken. I have some things for you and your mom. A casserole and salad for tonight, some muffins and fruit for the morning, and a few other little treats that are Theresa's favorites." She smiles, lips closed, head tilted to one side, still shielding her eyes from the sun.

"Th-thank you," Rosa manages to respond, completely baffled and not really knowing what else to say. Clumsily, she digs for her keys and says, "I'll unlock the door."

Soon, Theresa Colon and her mother stand in Rosa's kitchen, and the counter is covered with food. Mrs. Colon busies herself while Theresa's eyes rove. "Now, I'll just put a few of these things in the fridge while you girls chat. Heating instructions are on the casserole."

Theresa takes a step toward Rosa. "I'm really sorry about your dad," she says. "Everybody is really sorry."

As Rosa struggles to fully understand the weight of Theresa's apology, Mrs. Colon turns and fills the space between them with her words. "Those are such cute shoes! You'll have to tell Theresa where you got them."

And then it's Theresa's turn again. "Maybe we can go shopping together sometime." And then, as if forging the idea of a relationship, Theresa says, "Hey, I know. Let's take a selfie!" She rushes to Rosa's side, leaning closely and tilting her head. Rosa tries to smile. She tries to keep her eyes open. But inside, questions churn. She tries to imagine a friendship with Theresa Colon. Is that even possible? Is it something she even desires?

Her thoughts are interrupted by Theresa's mom. "I'm leaving some paperwork here on the counter. Rosa, this is very important." The smile fades. Her face is suddenly serious. "And I think it shows how important *you* are to us. To all of Foggy Creek." She takes a deep breath and bats her eyes as if attempting to hold back tears. "It's from the bank. And it's about a scholarship fund that has been set up for you."

Scholarship fund? Rosa marvels at how this day had taken an unexpected turn.

"You know, after your father's truck was found and we all knew that, well . . ." her voice trails off.

Theresa finishes the sentence for her. "So, Mr. Baron, Kyle's dad, suggested it, and my dad works at the bank. So, it just all came together really fast."

"Yes, sweetheart," Mrs. Colon adds. "We know what a good student you are, and we want you to have every opportunity." She reaches out and touches Rosa's shoulder. "So thoughtful of Mr. Baron, especially with everything he's going through right now."

"Thank you," Rosa manages to say. "I'll tell my mom."

"And you and your mom don't need to worry about meals for a while," Mrs. Colon says before parting. "We have a calendar set up for the next two months!"

After awkward hugs and sentimental words, Theresa and her mom climb back into the large white SUV. They drive away, leaving a cloud of dust hanging in the air like an echo of their presence.

That evening, Rosa sits on the couch eating Mrs. Colon's gooey mix of chicken, broccoli, and cheese while watching the evening news. The top story is again related to the sinkhole, but it seems to be only the local outlets who are still interested. The big news vans topped with satellite dishes have moved on. The crew of geophysicists had shrunk to two researchers and one truck.

However, the next part of the story catches Rosa off guard. A reporter speaks with the mayor. There is discussion of building some kind of monument in memory of Kyle Baron. "He is the descendent of some of our founding residents," the mayor reasons. "A brilliant young man with a bright future ahead of him, taken too soon. We want to honor him."

Back to the newsroom, the anchor mentions Luca Vieja, the picture of his abandoned truck once again floating next to her. A phone number appears on the screen. "Call this number if you'd like to donate to the scholarship fund set up for Mr. Vieja's teenage daughter."

Rosa sends a long thread of text messages to her mother. She knows that Marisol probably won't read them until her shift ends, but Rosa will be asleep by the time her mother gets home. This seems like the best way to let her know about the strange and unexpected developments of the afternoon.

Phone in hand, messages sent, Rosa dares to open social media. She holds her breath, not trusting Theresa's newly awakened sense of hospitality. But there it is—the selfie of the two of them. No words. Just two emojis: a broken heart and a care hug.

It's the comments that startle Rosa the most. No more venom. No more ridicule. It has all disappeared like the national news vans and their satellite dishes.

> *Poor Rosa. I can't imagine what she's going through.*
> *Theresa, UR such a good friend! So much love for Rosa!*
> *Rosa, if you're reading this, sit with us at lunch tomorrow!*
> *#friends #loveforRosa #FoggyCreekStrong*

Rosa closes the app. She puts the phone face down on the coffee table and cleans her dishes. She's glad the tide has turned, but can she trust it? Aren't these the same people who shunned her only hours ago? How can it all change so quickly?

But the bigger questions do not involve the opinions of others. The bigger questions reside within Rosa herself. Mr. White's words hang like dark shadows in her thoughts. *You have a gift a special connection to the spirit world. Nurture your gift, no matter what others think.*

She contemplates what seems to be two paths emerging before her. Should she lean into this new horizon? These newfound friendships? Forgive and forget? Accept and move on? Or should she follow the shadowy path that calls to her from the mist, from the darkness, from the mysterious voice?

Questions linger as Rosa crawls into bed. She hears Theresa's words on replay. *I'm really sorry. Everybody is really sorry.* And then Mr. White. *A gift. The spirit world.* And then the chill again. She suddenly wishes to dispel the words of Mr. White. She feels foolish for considering some connection to an abstract world when reality is so concrete. The sinkhole is real. The scientists are real. Even the friends seem real now.

After making sure her alarm is set, Rosa shakes her head, trying to rid it of the echoes. Content to live in the present and open herself to new friendships, to leave legends and lore behind, she falls into a deep sleep. But even in sleep, she cannot escape the world to which Mr. White had tied her. Because in sleep, it comes to visit her.

Bucky LeBlanc stands before her, slight build, brown eyes, dimple in his chin. So young. So innocent. So full of wonder. He speaks no words, and yet, she understands that he yearns for something. He longs to be acknowledged. To have his existence remembered by someone. To not be erased by a world that accepts and moves on without asking questions.

Rosa awakens with a start. The moon's glow creeps around the edges of her window shade. *It was a dream*, she told herself. *It was only a dream.*

As she walks to the kitchen for water, she laughs to herself. *There are no pictures of Bucky LeBlanc. I have no idea what he actually looked like.* She studies the shadowy forms on the countertop—a basket of muffins, a bowl of fruit, a tray of cookies. She opens the refrigerator. The casserole, the salad—they are real. They are concrete. Theresa and her mother are real. Their visit was real.

For the first time in weeks, Rosa begins to feel like a new sense of normal is possible. She smiles. She sips water. She tosses a couple of grapes in her mouth and concentrates on the shape, the texture, the sweetness.

Before returning to her room, she tiptoes once again to her mother's door. She peers through the crack in the door and sees Marisol sleeping, a box of tissues by her bedside. *She wept*, Rosa thinks. *But maybe this time they are good tears.*

And then she returns to her own room, resolved to move forward. To sleep peacefully. To awaken to a new day with acceptance and forgiveness and friendship. But as she sits on the edge of her bed, somewhere in the distance, the voice calls to her again. *Innocent blood.*

Rosa rushes to the window and opens the shade. No longer fearful, she acknowledges her anger at this intrusion. And yet, she cannot ignore it. The voice comes again, from the east, from the misty distance. *Innocent blood.* It pulls her, like the moon pulls the tide. And she knows that it will not leave her alone until she faces it.

And so, Rosa quickly changes into jeans and a T-shirt. She puts on her bargain sneakers and almost laughs at the memory. *Those are such cute shoes.* And Theresa following with *maybe we can go shopping together.* But there is no time to laugh. Rosa is determined to find the source of this voice and rid herself of it forever.

She slides the window open quietly and takes one careful look back toward her closed bedroom door. She climbs through the open window. She steps onto the rocky ground. She lowers the window behind her, careful to make sure it remains unlocked. And she begins her journey toward the voice.

Again, she hears the words. *Innocent blood.* Her hands tremble, but her feet are sure, her mind completely awake. The voice grows louder as she moves toward it. She loses track of time and regrets not bringing her phone, but there is no turning back. She continues to move through the fields, along the roadside, into the wilderness, toward the mist.

Finally, Rosa is standing at the edge of the abandoned oil field. She ignores the signs, the barriers, the caution tape. She continues to move forward across this field of memories. Over the ground that once vibrated, alive with music. *World Renowned Terrance Brown. New subwoofers. Gotta love the sound!*

Step by step, she continues through the memory of that night. Theresa saying *Don't you two make a cute couple!* Manny's reply, *We're just friends.* And then his dancing. His crazy dancing.

Still moving, she passes the spot where she stood when Kyle Baron walked toward her, his eyes locked on hers. *I didn't think you'd come.* His surprise. His delight. Her heart racing. And then the dance. He was real. He was solid. They swayed together.

Finally, *Go long!* Rick Santini's voice shatters her dreamy reverie. She looks around, suddenly aware that she is dangerously close to the sinkhole. Suddenly out of her own head and back in this desolate space.

She looks ahead, where the mist rises and mixes with moonlight. And then, once more, the voice. *Innocent blood.* So close this time. And there, in the mist, she sees a figure arise. The form is slight, thin. She knows she must confront it. So she steps closer, being cautious, but unwilling to be ignored.

And as she approaches, the figure turns. Moonlight falls across him. The brown eyes, the dimple in his chin. It is Bucky LeBlanc. The Bucky LeBlanc of her dream. But how? She is wide awake. She feels the warm earth beneath her feet, the humid air clinging to her arms and face.

His eyes meet hers, and he smiles. Sort of. Not a warm or happy smile. Just a sad but satisfied grin. She reaches her hand out, not close enough to touch him, but close enough to say *I see you. I acknowledge you. I know what happened.* And while her hand still hangs in the air, those statements vibrating from her silent consciousness, he begins to transform.

Rosa stares, wide-eyed, trying to make a mental recording of this experience. Right before her, Bucky LeBlanc's face ages. His brown eyes turn gray, and the color swirls within them like gathering storm clouds. Rosa stands frozen, horrified at the recognition.

"Mr. White." No other words will form. Rosa stands, feet planted on solid ground. She drinks in the humid air and steadies her nerves. *Breathe in peace . . .*

The now-familiar form of her history teacher seems to hover more than stand, no more than twenty feet before her. He lowers his head, but to her relief, he makes no move in her direction. He is wrapped in a thick fog. Moonlight pierces the mist and casts an eerie glow upon his face.

"Rosa," he says. "Finally, you've come. I need to explain."

Rosa takes a step back and readies herself to run. Her heart races and her mind whirls. *Has he been calling to me all this time? Am I part of some sinister plan?*

"Please, don't go!" he shouts. His hand reaches toward her through the fog. "I must explain!"

Rosa steadies herself with another deep breath, and then she responds. "Okay, I'll listen. But don't come any closer." She's surprised by the strength she hears in her own voice.

"I won't come any closer. Just hear me out," he pleads.

"So, you are Bucky LeBlanc. I see that much. What more is there to know?" Suddenly, Rosa feels foolish for not putting this together sooner. LeBlanc. She's taken enough French to know that it translates as "the White." Why hadn't she figured this out? And yet, how could this even be real? Rosa's mind whirls, and her feet remain poised to run, but prepared to stay.

"My only crime was my youth, and the ignorance that came with it. I had hopes. I had dreams. This land was the key to everything I ever wanted. And if I had only known about the oil, if I had only realized." He drops his head and seems to battle within himself before raising it again, steady and composed.

"When I went to see Horatio Baron, I was hasty. Impetuous. I realize that now. I should have taken my time. I should have learned what I had. But that doesn't excuse his behavior! He took advantage of me! His greed cost me my life!" A fury seems to ignite within him, and the mist begins to swirl in sync with the storm clouds in his eyes.

"He took my life, Rosa. He took the land. He took the oil and the wealth it brought. And he buried me here, in this very spot. And nothing ever happened. There was no consequence. I disappeared. He won. End of story. But you must understand. I couldn't let it end that way. There had to be a reckoning."

Rosa begins to follow his trail of logic,

but then she remembers Kyle. His warm grin. The way he would sling his sandy hair to the side. The dance beneath the moonlight. And suddenly, anger rises within her.

"Kyle Baron never did anything to harm you! He's innocent! Don't you see?" Rosa is amazed by the force of her words. Her breathing is shallow, and her heart races. But she stands her ground, and her face remains stern.

"Justice had to be served," Mr. White continues. "It was the only way Bucky could—I could—rest in peace. You must understand."

Suddenly Rosa is overcome by emotion. Her father. What about her father? How did he figure into this reckoning?

"I know what you're thinking," Mr. White continues. "And it's why I've called to you. I had to apologize. Your father wasn't supposed to be here. This was not prepared for him. He was collateral damage."

"Collateral damage?!" she shouts. "You excuse his death as just an accident in your grand scheme of reckoning? He was my father!

And you have taken him from me!" Mr. White moves toward her, and she immediately raises a hand. "Don't come any closer." Her voice is low and threatening now, and fury fills her eyes.

Mr. White stops. "I'm sorry, Rosa," he says. "I'm truly sorry." And with those words, his gray eyes morph to a rich brown, a dimple forms in his chin, and his face becomes that of the young and innocent dreamer from Rosa's dream.

"Goodbye, Rosa," he says. And he fades into the mist, leaving her to stand alone in the moonlight.

Rosa exits the school bus, carrying with her a mix of emotions. There is relief. That she made it home. That she was able to climb back through the window and into her bed without her mother ever waking. There is anger. How can she face Mr. White now, knowing what he has done? How can she carry this secret inside of her? And yet, how can she ever share it with anyone else?

"Rosa, wait up!" she turns to see Theresa Colon waving, running toward her. She stops and allows Theresa to catch up.

"Hey," Rosa manages, unsure if the meek Theresa who stood in her house only yesterday is the person who stands before her today. Or now that she's away from her mother, will the old Theresa return?

"I'm so glad I caught you," Theresa says, nearly out of breath from the short jog. "Listen, first I want to apologize. I know I made up the whole rumor thing about you conjuring up a sinkhole. It sounds crazy to even say it." Theresa looks at the ground, her face draining of color. "It's so ridiculous." And then a chuckle. She looks up. "I mean, if you were going to conjure a hole in the ground as a way to get rid of somebody, I'm sure I would be the one in the sinkhole, right?"

Rosa smiles, but she doesn't respond. She had to admit, the girl's logic made sense.

Theresa continues. "Look, the girls and I want you to eat lunch with us. Please! Do you know where we sit?"

Do I know where you sit? Everyone knows where you sit! Rosa thinks the words but keeps them from being voiced. "Yeah," she says. "But I usually sit with Manny—"

"That's okay!" Theresa smiles brightly. "Bring him with you!" And then she grins and leans close. "All the girls think he's kind of cute. It'll be fun."

"Okay, I'll see," Rosa begins. But Theresa has already turned and moved on to the next person on her agenda.

As Rosa enters the front of the school, she sees that a glass trophy case has been transformed into a memorial honoring Kyle Baron. There are photos of his smiling face through the years, trophies from his various athletic achievements, his football jersey, his helmet. Tears form in Rosa's eyes, but she knows she cannot make space for this kind of emotion.

So, she forges ahead to her locker, knowing the next step is to face Mr. White. She steels her nerves. She steadies her fingers, concentrates on her combination, and opens her locker.

"Rosa," Manny's voice comes from behind her.

"Hey," she answers. She attempts a smile but fears it doesn't look genuine. Is this hostile territory, or are they still friends? She can't be sure.

But Manny gives her that familiar half-smile, and says, "So, Theresa tells me you're sitting with her little club at lunch today. And I'm invited?" He raises his eyebrows, and Rosa is relieved.

"Yeah," she says. "It sounds like that's the plan," and she laughs as Manny launches into a celebratory dance.

They walked together to first period, and she's glad to have Manny as a buffer when she enters the classroom. To her surprise, they are greeted by the principal, who is hastily sending students to their seats and handing out busywork.

"Class," the principal announces, "we have a bit of a crisis this morning. Mr. White did not show up for his morning duty. We've tried calling and his number seems to have been disconnected. I've sent someone to check on him. It's all so strange." Flustered and suddenly regaining her sense of discretion, the principal follows that flood of information by saying, "I don't know why I'm telling you all this. I'm sorry. TMI, as you kids say. Right?"

Throughout the day, Rosa's life seems to fall back into place. She feels restored. Things are not the same, but the new normal seems comfortable, and she is lulled into a sense of security. A sense of moving on. A sense of peace.

That evening, she and her mother dine on another casserole provided by the concerned citizens of Foggy Creek. Marisol is eager to share news with Rosa. She has been offered a job at the bank. It's an entry-level position, she explains, and she has a lot to learn. But she is beaming with excitement. "It means I will work only one job. I will be here with you in the evenings. I start next week!"

Mother and daughter laugh. They hug. They celebrate. They find peace in the new normal. Still, Marisol must rush off to the diner. She has given her notice, but her shift has not yet been covered. So, Rosa is left alone once more.

As she readies herself for bed, her mind replays the events of the past twenty-four hours. Bucky LeBlanc, Mr. White, Manny, Theresa, her mom. So much has happened. She feels like she's been on a dark journey, and she's thankful to see a light ahead. Some hope for a new tomorrow.

And then a twinge of guilt pierces her happiness. She picks up the frame that holds her father's image. Moving forward requires letting go. She looks into his kind eyes and watches as her own salty tear drops onto the glass. She replaces the picture on the bedside table. The tear rolls down the glass, as if rolling down Luca's own cheek.

Rosa stands at the open window and looks out into the quiet night. The full moon hovers above the seemingly endless landscape. *It was a mistake.* The words echo in her mind and sting her heart. *Collateral damage.* More tears fall from her eyes. *Breathe in peace*, she reminds herself.

And there, alone at the window, Rosa looks to the east and voices the words, "Innocent blood." Before she has a chance to lower the shade, to shut out the world, to close this chapter and find sleep, a new chill creeps into her room.

A fine mist rises in the distance, and from across the rugged fields and narrow roads, an echo answers her. But it is not her own voice returning, and it is not the voice of Bucky LeBlanc. This time it is the voice of Luca Vieja.

"Innocent blood!"

ABOUT THE AUTHOR

Susan Koehler LOVES books! She loves to read them and she loves to write them. Susan is the author of five nonfiction books for children, and two novels for young readers. She has also written several professional resource books for teachers. As a veteran educator, Susan loves to work with students and teachers. You can learn more about Susan's books, author visits, and writing workshops at susankoehlerwrites.com.